Calico's Ghost
A Blackbear the Pirate Adventure

More Blackbear the Pirate Adventures:

Blackbear the Pirate
The Search for Captain Ben

Calico's Ghost

A Blackbear the Pirate Adventure

Written by
Steve Buckley

Illustrated by
Ruth Palmer

SeaStory Press
Key West, Florida

To Learn More About Captain Blackbear and His Crew
visit blackbearthepirate.com

Calico's Ghost, A Blackbear the Pirate Adventure

© 2012 by Steve Buckley

Printed in Hong Kong.

ISBN 978-1-936818-30-3

LCCN 2012949700

SeaStory Press
305 Whitehead St. #1
Key West. Florida 33040
www.seastorypress.com

Dedication

For Joseph Stephen:
You can always find me right here,
between these pages.

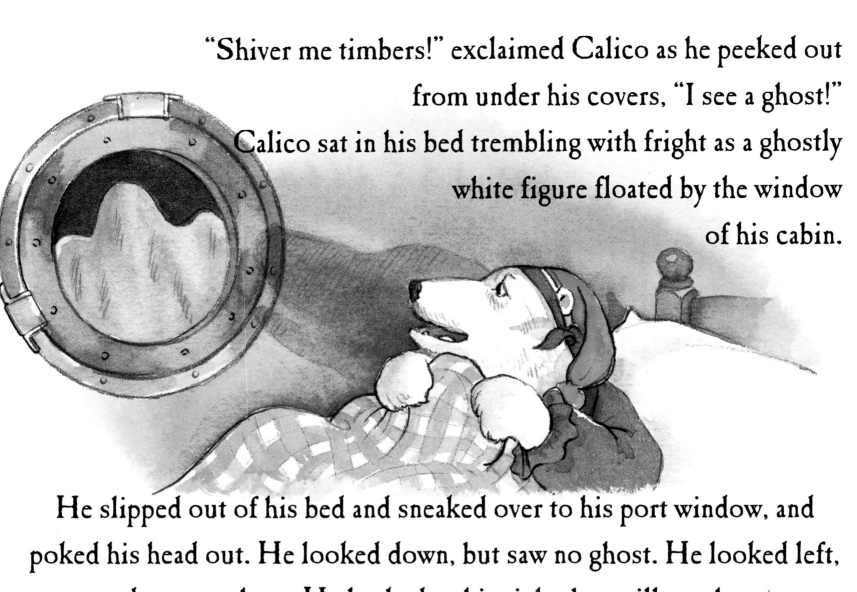

"Shiver me timbers!" exclaimed Calico as he peeked out from under his covers, "I see a ghost!" Calico sat in his bed trembling with fright as a ghostly white figure floated by the window of his cabin.

He slipped out of his bed and sneaked over to his port window, and poked his head out. He looked down, but saw no ghost. He looked left, and saw no ghost. He looked to his right, but still no ghost.

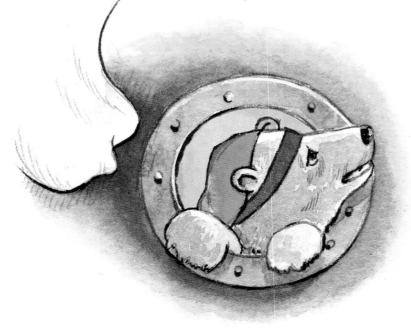

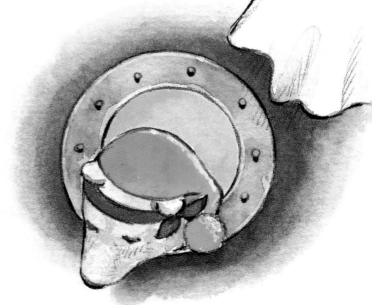

As he let out a sigh of relief he declared,
"I must have been having a nightmare!"

Calico was settling back in his bed
when he looked up and found the ghost
floating right above him. He was frozen with fear.

"What do, do, do you, you, you want?"

Calico stammered.

"Ohhhhh Calico,
Ohhhhh Calico,
I ... want ...YOU!"

"Ahhhhhhhhhhhhh!" screamed Calico as he leaped up out of bed
and ran towards the door.

He raced down the hall calling,
"Blackbear, Captain Blackbear,
come quick!"

Blackbear the Pirate was sleeping soundly until he heard Calico calling his name. The door to his room flew open as Calico went tumbling into Blackbear's room.

"What are you doing you salty old sea bear?" asked Blackbear the Pirate, "What are you yelling about?"

All of the noise had awakened the rest of the crew. They gathered at
Blackbear's door listening as Calico tried to explain,
"It's the Annie, Captain, it's the Annie!"
"The Annie is haunted!" he finally said as he collapsed onto
a chair beside the bed.

"Haunted?!" grumbled Barty, the
wisest member of the crew.
"What makes you think the Annie is haunted?"
"I saw a ghost, in my cabin," assured Calico,
"Follow me and I'll show you!"

"There are no such things as ghosts," Barty told Calico,
as they headed back to Calico's room.
"Don't be too sure of that," said Blackbear the Pirate.

Blackbear and the crew arrived at Calico's cabin and looked inside
to find the room in a wreck.
"What a mess!" declared Bonnie, "What happened in here?"
"I guess I bumped into a few things," admitted Calico,
"But it's that ghost's fault!"
"Ghost indeed!" doubted Barty,
"You just had a bad dream," added Izzy Paws.

Izzy Paws, Bonnie and Barty joined in to help Calico put his cabin back in order, while Blackbear went to find LeKidd and Pawly.

He stepped out onto the deck of his great ship, the Annie, and made his way over to the stairway that led to the upper deck. He stopped to listen when he heard laughter coming from behind the stairs.

"You make a fine ghost, to be sure," LeKidd told Pawly the
Parrot. "Flying around with that sheet over you sure scared that
salty old sea bear good!"
"Ohhhhh Calico, Ohhhhh Calico," moaned
LeKidd as he started to laugh.

Blackbear the Pirate had found Calico's ghost!
Pretending he had just come out on deck, Blackbear called out,
"LeKidd, Pawly, I'm here to take the next watch."
"Ahoy there maties, go get some sleep," offered
Blackbear the Pirate as he eyed them carefully.

"Aye aye, Captain," replied LeKidd as he scampered down
into the Annie with Pawly right behind him.

As soon as they are out of sight, Blackbear went into action. He lit a lantern and raised a signal flag, and then went and told the crew to come to his cabin. Everyone but LeKidd and Pawly, that is!

LeKidd was just closing his eyes when he was startled
by a moaning noise, "Oooooooooooo!"
"Did you hear that?" he asked Pawly the Parrot,
who was sitting on his perch beside the bed.

They heard another moan come from just outside the door, "Oooooooooooooooo!"

LeKidd climbed out of bed and went over and opened the door
to find a ghostly pirate hovering in front of him.
"I'm not scared of you," declared LeKidd as he turned to Pawly,
"It's just Calico trying to get us back."

LeKidd and Pawly headed down the hall to Blackbear's cabin
with the ghostly pirate following behind.

They pushed open the door to find Blackbear and the rest of the crew seated around the room. Everyone, but Calico.
As LeKidd and Pawly entered the room Barty asked,
"What is the matter LeKidd, why aren't you asleep?"

"Because Calico is pretending to be a ghost and trying to scare us," he explained as the ghostly pirate entered the room.

"Oooooooooooo," moaned the ghost.

"Oh my!" exclaimed Bonnie, "Aren't you afraid of the ghost?"

"No, it's just Calico." claimed LeKidd.

"It's just Calico!" squawked Pawly the Parrot.

"Aye there matey, if that's Calico then who is this?" asked Blackbear the Pirate pointing to Calico as he stepped out from behind the door. "Calico!" cried LeKidd as he jumped back, bumping into the ghostly spirit.

LeKidd slowly turned around to find the ghostly pirate staring down at him.

His mouth dropped open and his eyes widened as the ghost leaned down coming nose to nose with him,

"Ooooooooooooo, BOO!"

"Ahhhhhhhhhhh!" screamed LeKidd as he ran out of the room and raced up to the deck of the Annie with the ghost and the others following behind.

When they arrived on deck, they found LeKidd and Pawly hiding behind the stairs, "It's okay to come out," assured Blackbear the Pirate, "There is someone I want you to meet."

"Captain Edward D. Teach at your service," offered the pirate ghost.

"Wow!" exclaimed the crew, "A real ghost!"

"Until next time old friend," said Blackbear the Pirate as he gave
a farewell salute to Captain Teach.

They all waved goodbye as Captain Teach's
ghostly ship faded into the night.
"What an exciting night!" exclaimed Bonnie.
"A little too exciting!" grumbled Barty.

"Is there something you would like to say to Calico?"
Blackbear asked LeKidd.
"I'm sorry Calico," replied LeKidd,
"Pawly and I meant no harm."
"Aye there maties, no harm done," replied Calico.

Everyone smiled, and then they all moaned "Oooooooooooo"
as they swooped around the deck and pretended to be ghosts.
"Settle down now everyone," said Blackbear the Pirate, "It's very late
and tomorrow we set sail for our next great adventure."
"Hooray!" cheered the crew.